any

The
Spider Gnomes

First published in Great Britain by
HarperCollins Children's Books 2011
HarperCollins Children's Books is a division of
HarperCollins*Publishers* Ltd,
77-85 Fulham Palace Road, Hammersmith, London W6 8JB

Visit us on the web at
www.harpercollins.co.uk

1

SOPHIE AND THE SHADOW WOODS : THE SPIDER GNOMES
Text copyright © Linda Chapman and Lee Weatherly 2011
Illustrations © Katie Wood 2011

Linda Chapman and Lee Weatherly assert the moral right
to be identified as the authors of this work.

ISBN 978-0-00-741167-2

Printed and bound in England by
Clays Ltd, St Ives plc

Mixed Sources
Product group from well-managed
forests and other controlled sources
www.fsc.org Cert no. SW-COC-001806
© 1996 Forest Stewardship Council

FSC

FSC is a non-profit international organisation established to promote the
responsible management of the world's forests. Products carrying the FSC
label are independently certified to assure consumers that they come
from forests that are managed to meet the social, economic and
ecological needs of present and future generations.

Find out more about HarperCollins and the environment at
www.harpercollins.co.uk/green

More

Sophie
AND THE
Shadow Woods

adventures:

The Goblin King
The Swamp Boggles

Linda Chapman & Lee Weatherly

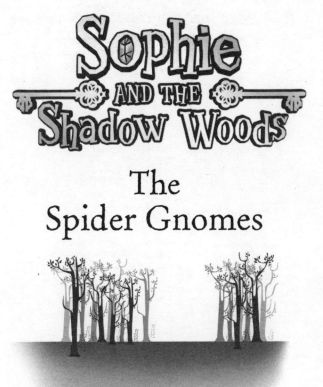

Sophie AND THE Shadow Woods

The Spider Gnomes

Illustrated by Katie Wood

HarperCollins *Children's Books*

Contents

The Shadow Woods...

Very few people ever enter the Shadow Woods. The crooked trees press closely together, their branches reaching out like skeletons' arms. Strange whispers echo through the quiet air, and eyes seem to watch from the shadows. Anyone who does go in soon leaves, their skin prickling with fear. For these woods are like no others. Hidden deep within them is a gateway to the Shadow Realm – a dark and chaotic world where all the mischief-making creatures like goblins, boggles and trolls live.

Many hundreds of years ago, the Shadow Realm

creatures could pass freely between our world and theirs, but they caused so much trouble that it was decided the gateway between the two worlds must be shut for good. Yet no one knew how to do this, until a locksmith with magical powers made an iron key and then slotted a gem from the Shadow Realm into its handle. The secret had been found! The locksmith forced as many shadow creatures as he could back into their own world and locked the gateway firmly behind them.

From that day on, the locksmith became the Guardian of the Gateway, watching over the precious key and stopping the few shadow creatures left in this world from causing too much trouble. As he grew old he passed his powers on to

his grandson, who in turn passed the powers on to his. For hundreds of years, the Guardianship has passed down from grandparent to grandchild, and the gate has always remained safely shut.

But now for the first time, disaster looms. The shadow creatures have stolen the iron key! Luckily, there was no gem in its handle when it was taken, but there are six gems from the Shadow Realm hidden somewhere in our world. If the shadow creatures find any of them, they'll be able to slot them into the key and open the gateway, letting hordes of villainous creatures loose to cause mayhem and trouble.

Only one girl stands in their way... and her name is Sophie Smith.

1

The New Clue

'm a Swamp Boggle and I'm coming to get you!"

Sophie peered cautiously round the tree trunk as the voice grew closer. There he was! She jerked back again, hoping he hadn't seen her. *Wait*, she told herself. *Let him get nearer...*

She counted to ten. Her fingers tightened on the trigger. *Now!*

Darting out from behind the tree, she lifted her bright orange mega-soaker and fired a jet of water straight at Sam, her best friend. "Got you, you stinky Swamp Boggle!" she yelled.

Sam counter attacked, shooting water back at her. Sophie dodged away, diving to the ground and rolling over before leaping to her feet again.

"Hi-YA!" Dropping her mega-soaker, she jumped into the air, kicking out with her right foot in a tae kwon do move. She timed it closely because she didn't want to hurt Sam really. He staggered backwards in surprise as her foot missed him by just a few centimetres.

"Whoa!" He tripped and landed on the grass.

"Ha!" said Sophie, dusting her hands down.

"Don't mess with me, Swamp Boggle!"

She didn't get to gloat for long. Sam pulled the trigger on his mega-soaker, drenching her legs with water. "Gotcha!"

Sophie squealed. Leaping up again, Sam chased her round his garden until their water pistols finally ran out and they both flopped on to the patio. Sophie's blonde ponytail was dripping and Sam's red hair was flattened against his head.

"I'm wet through!" Sam panted.

"Me too, but it was fun!" Sophie's green eyes shone. "Isn't it nice just to do something normal for a change."

Sam grinned. "You mean fighting Ink Cap Goblins and Swamp Boggles isn't normal?"

"I suppose it *is* normal for us now," said Sophie. A week ago, on her tenth birthday, she'd discovered that she was the Guardian of a magical gateway hidden deep in the woods behind her house. Her grandfather, the previous Guardian, had explained she had to stop the shadow creatures from ever opening it. Sam was the only person apart from her grandpa who knew the secret. Sophie was very glad he was helping her.

Sam stretched his legs out. "What do you think Ug will do next to try to find the gems?" Ug, the King of the Ink Cap Goblins, had stolen the key to the gateway and was trying to find one of the six hidden shadow gems. The key wouldn't work without one of them.

"Whatever it is, I bet it's something horrible," answered Sophie. She touched the pouch under her jeans, where she carried the two gems she and Sam had found so far. There were still four others hidden around the town of Upper Gately, where they lived – and they *had* to find them before Ug did! But who knew what plan he'd come up with next? After she and Sam had defeated him, he'd sent the scary Swamp Boggles to try to find one of the gems.

Sophie shivered, remembering how they had just barely got away from the slimy creatures. She hoped they wouldn't have to deal with any more shadow creatures... but she had a feeling that they would!

She reached for the leather notebook that was lying on the patio behind her. *The Shadow Files* was written in fading gold letters on the front. It contained notes made by the past Guardians on all the different shadow creatures they'd encountered.

"If Ug sends another creature after the gems, it could be any of these," she said, flicking through its pages. Slime Imps, Fire Goblins, Wolf Trolls – each looked worse than the last! "Let's read the clue for the red gem again." *The*

Shadow Files had clues to help the new Guardian find the gems. Earlier that morning, she and Sam had discovered the third clue, hidden in tiny letters at the bottom of the entry on Snake Sprites. "We *must* be able to work it out."

Sam turned to the correct page and read:

"Hours and minutes
Near clouds and sky
The red gem is hidden
Way up high."

"Any ideas yet?" Sophie looked at him hopefully. Sam was really brainy, and excellent at working stuff out. But this time he seemed as stumped as she was.

"No, none. The gem's hidden somewhere

high up… but how can hours and minutes be near the sky? It doesn't make any sense."

"Let's go back to my house," suggested Sophie. "Maybe Grandpa will know what the new clue means."

As Sam picked up the mega-soakers, Sophie noticed a long line of spiders a few metres away, marching across the patio. "Hey, look at all the spiders!" she exclaimed.

"That's weird," said Sam, staring down at them. "Spiders normally hide when it's hot outside. They like cool, dry places." Sophie raised her eyebrows at him, and he shrugged. "What? Spiders are fascinating creatures."

"Mmmmm, *really* fascinating!" she teased.

"They are, actually. Spiders are cool," Sam informed her. "Did you know some spiders can jump up to fifty times their own length? Some of them use their web silk to make lassoes to catch prey, and others make parachutes with it." His forehead creased as he looked at the spiders again. "I wonder why so many of them are out at the same time though?"

Sophie shrugged, bored of the spiders. "Maybe one of them's having a spider party, and texted his friends to say come and have some flies! Come on, let's go."

She went to the back door. Taking one last puzzled look at the spiders, Sam followed her.

Deep in the Shadow Woods stood King Ug, the leader of the Ink Cap Goblins. His ivy crown rested wonkily on his dome-shaped head and his white flaky skin was covered with black blotches. He was talking to two squat figures in the shadows.

"Well? Do you think you can get one?" he demanded.

"Yessss," one of the figures hissed, waving four of its eight legs. "We shall find a shadow gem, no matter what."

"Those idiot Swamp Boggles said the same thing," snorted King Ug. "They failed me. Numskulls!"

There was the sound of snapping jaws. "Ah,

but *we* shall not fail you. We know how important it is that we shadow creatures all serve you, King Ug – you are the Keeper of the Key!"

King Ug smiled proudly. The key to the gate hung round his chest, and he reached up and touched it, feeling the empty space where a shadow gem needed to go. "How will you manage to get into the town unseen?" he demanded.

There was the sound of leg joints cracking. "We have many spiessss with many eyessss," said one of the figures. A line of tiny spiders marched past on the ground. "They will search the humans' town and find a gem for us, and when they do we shall fetch it and bring it here. Nothing shall stop usss!"

"Excellent!" chortled King Ug. He adjusted his crown. "I can see it was extremely clever of me to call on the Spider Gnomes for help. When you succeed, the gem will be mine and I shall finally open the gate." His small black eyes gleamed as he imagined the fun that millions of shadow creatures would have, wreaking havoc in the human world.

All he needed was one small gem...

2

Spider Invasion

"OK, this is really weird. There are even *more* spiders here," Sam said as he and Sophie walked towards her house. They lived on the same road, Sam near the town and Sophie at the end, in a house that bordered on to the Shadow Woods.

Sophie groaned. "Forget the

spiders, Sam! Race you to my house! Last one there is a squashed bug!"

She charged off with Sam pounding after her. Sophie just managed to beat him. "Hi, Mrs B!" she called as they tumbled in through the front door.

Sophie's parents were archaeologists and were away working for a few months, so Grandpa and the housekeeper, Mrs B, were looking after Sophie and her twin brother, Anthony.

Mrs B was in the kitchen. "Hello, you two! Come and meet Nigel. I've just collected him."

Sophie smiled as she remembered. "Nigel's the parrot Mrs B is looking after for a few weeks," she explained as she and Sam kicked off their trainers. "She's keeping him here. Let's go and see!"

They hurried into the kitchen. On the table

26

was a large birdcage with a grey parrot inside. He had a curved black beak and white feathers round his eyes. Seeing Sam and Sophie, he walked sideways along his perch.

"Isn't he beautiful?" cooed Mrs B. "Say hello, Nigel."

The parrot put his head coyly to one side. "Hello, Nigel."

Sophie grinned.

"No, no, just say *hello*," Mrs B told the parrot. "Go on."

"Hello. Go on," the parrot gabbled.

"How about *hiya*?" suggested Sam. He turned to the parrot. "Hiya!"

"*Fire!*" the parrot screeched. "Fire, fire, FIRE!" He bobbed excitedly up and down.

Sophie giggled. "What about Pretty Polly? Can you say Pretty Polly?"

"You're a wally! You're a wally!" cackled the parrot.

Mrs B blinked as Sophie and Sam fell about laughing. "Oh, dear! I'm not sure he should be saying *that*!"

"He's brilliant!" cried Sophie. "We should record him and show him to everyone at school." She saw her grandpa's mobile phone on the side. "Here. Let's give it a go with this."

She tried using the camera on the phone to film Nigel, but the parrot didn't seem to like the idea. He screeched loudly every time she held the phone up in front of him.

"Wow, is he noisy or what?" said Sam, raising his voice over the din.

"I think you'd better stop now, Sophie-duckie," said Mrs B. She covered the parrot's cage with a dark cloth and Nigel fell silent. "That should calm him down. It makes him think it's night-time, so he'll go to sleep."

Sam nudged Sophie. "You're a wally!" he squawked. They both started giggling again.

Just then there was a yell and Anthony, Sophie's twin brother, shot in through the door. Like Sophie, he had blonde hair, but his eyes were pale blue instead of green.

"There are spiders everywhere in the house,

Mrs B!" he cried. His voice shook. "They keep coming into my room through the window, and they're on the landing and in the hall. There's a massive one on the stairs!"

Spiders again! Sophie and Sam looked at each other in surprise. "We've got loads at my house too," said Sam.

"And we saw some more on the way here," added Sophie.

"Oh, dear, there must be an infestation. Here, take some of this." Mrs B went to the cupboard under the stairs and passed Anthony a can of lemon furniture polish. "Spray it on your windowsill."

Anthony frowned. "But I want to get rid of the spiders, not clean my room!"

"Yes, but this will keep the spiders out," Mrs B told him. "Spiders don't like strong flavours

30

like lemon or eucalyptus, so if you spray a scented furniture polish on the windowsill they won't cross it."

"They also love cardboard," chipped in Sam, "so make sure you don't leave any cardboard boxes lying around."

Anthony rolled his eyes. "Trust *you* to be a freaky spider expert, geek-brain!"

"Shut up!" Sophie said angrily. It was OK for her to tease Sam, but not Anthony. He and his friends were always picking on Sam at school. "Least Sam's not afraid of spiders like you. Chick-chick-chick-chick chicken!"

Anthony scowled and kicked out at her.

"Stop that, both of you," Mrs B said. "Anthony, go on – take the spray upstairs and put some on your window ledge."

"Wish I had a spray that would work on you

two," Anthony muttered to Sophie and Sam as he passed. Sophie pulled a face at him.

"Now, I wonder why there aren't any spiders in here," said Mrs B, looking around the kitchen.

"It's probably because of Nigel," Sam told her. "Spiders *really* don't like birds, because birds eat them."

"Maybe we should get more parrots then," suggested Sophie, lifting the corner of the cover over Nigel's cage.

"FIRE!" he shrieked, flapping his wings.

Mrs B quickly pulled the cover back down. "Maybe not! Now, I suppose I'd better go and help Anthony with all these spiders." Picking up a broom, she bustled out.

Alone, Sophie and Sam looked at each other. "What do you reckon is going on?" said Sam in a low voice.

Sophie shook her head. "I don't know!" Just then she caught sight of her grandpa through the window. He was standing by the fence that separated the garden from the wood. "Come on! Maybe Grandpa'll know!"

They hurried outside. Sophie's grandpa was staring at the ground and scratching his short grey hair. He didn't look like most grandfathers and was very fit – he went running and swimming every day.

"Look at this!" breathed Grandpa as they came running up. "Hundreds of spiders – and they're all coming out of the Shadow Woods!"

Sophie's scalp prickled as she stared down at the long line of spiders moving through the grass. "They're everywhere inside – and at Sam's house too."

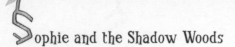

Grandpa gazed grimly into the woods. "Something is going on with the shadow creatures. I just know it is."

Sophie grinned, unable to resist. "Your spider sense is tingling, Grandpa!" she said, thinking of Spider-Man.

Sam sniggered too, but Grandpa didn't look amused. "Sophie, this is no—"

"Laughing matter. I know," sighed Sophie. Grandpa was always telling her that she didn't take things seriously enough. He'd been amazed when she'd become the Guardian. The job of protecting the gateway had never gone to a girl before, and Grandpa had assumed that Anthony would be the next Guardian after him. But the magic had chosen Sophie instead – and now she was determined to prove that she was the right choice.

"Should we go into the woods and see where the spiders are coming from?" she said eagerly.

Grandpa shook his head. "It's too risky. We

should look through *The Shadow Files* first, and see if anything like this has ever happened before." He fixed her with a stare. "You have a worrying tendency to just go jumping into things, child. Remember: think before you act! Now, have you got *The Shadow Files* with you?"

Sam nodded and took the book out of his bag. "Oh – and we found the clue for the red gem!" He opened the page and showed it to Grandpa.

"Excellent!" Grandpa read it over quickly. "So, have you worked it out?"

"Um… no," Sophie admitted.

Grandpa scowled. "Well, then, what are you doing, standing round here talking? You two get to work on the clue, and I'll read through *The Shadow Files* and see if it says anything

about spiders." Taking the book, he strode inside.

Sophie let out a breath. "He so wishes I wasn't the Guardian."

"Well, he's nuts. You're brilliant at it. Anthony would be rubbish," said Sam comfortingly. "Can you just picture it? *'Eek! A spider! Help me, help me!'*" he squeaked in a high, frightened voice.

Sophie laughed, feeling better. "I guess we'd better think about the clue now," she said.

But she didn't want to stand around, thinking about clues. She wanted to do something exciting!

"Maybe we could just take a *little* look in the woods," she said, gazing into the tangled trees. "To find out where the spiders are coming from."

"Your grandpa said not to," Sam reminded her.

"I know, but..." Sophie looked at him hopefully. "We might find out something useful, and it'll be loads more fun than sitting here working out the clue. Come on, which is it to be? Go to the woods or stay here?"

Sam grinned. "No contest. Let's go!"

3

A Curtain of Cobwebs

he woods pressed in around Sophie and Sam. The leaves overhead blocked out the light, and they could hear strange rustlings in the undergrowth. They headed down a path, fighting through brambles and stepping over tree roots.

"How are you feeling?"

Sam whispered to Sophie.

Part of Sophie's Guardian magic meant that whenever a shadow creature was near, a tingling feeling would run through her, and she'd suddenly become super-fast and super-strong. It was what she liked best about being the Guardian. It was amazing doing the moves she practised in her tae kwon do classes, but with the magic flowing through her!

"I just feel normal so far," she whispered back.

They continued along the twisting path, looking at the stream of spiders.

"Maybe they're leaving because they're scared of something," Sophie suggested.

"They don't look scared," Sam pointed out. "They're moving quite slowly, marching, almost. It's like they've got a purpose—" He

broke off as he and Sophie stepped into a clearing. "Wow! Look at those massive trees!"

Sophie was already staring at them. They were huge! Their trunks were as wide as a car and they seemed to reach all the way up to the sky. "I never knew there were trees like that in here!"

The Shadow Woods was such a spooky place – you never knew quite what you would find in it.

Suddenly she felt a familiar tingling in her toes. "Sam! My Guardian powers are starting!"

He gulped. "That means there must be a shadow creature around!"

Sophie looked at the trees. She felt like she was being pulled towards them. "This way!"

The tingling grew stronger as they headed in the direction of the towering tree trunks. Suddenly Sophie stopped. There was a giant cobweb about four times her height stretched

42

between two of the trees! A row of small spiders was marching out from underneath it, heading towards the town.

"Look!" she exclaimed. "I wonder what's behind that cobweb?"

Sam looked queasy. "Um, a pretty big spider?"

Sophie lifted her chin. "Well, take cover, Incey Wincey, here we come!"

"Sophie! Wait!" Sam clutched her sleeve as she started forward. "It might be really dangerous."

"But that's where the spiders are coming from! I've got to find out what's behind that web." Sophie saw the worry in his eyes. "Why don't you wait here if you want?"

"No way! I'm not letting you go through there alone," said Sam fiercely. "If you're going

to be eaten by a giant spider, I'll be eaten too!"
Suddenly there was a dropping movement from the trees behind them, and two long hisses rang out.

"Whoa!" Sam yelled as he and Sophie swung round. Sophie stared, her blood running cold.

Two horrible-looking shadow creatures stood facing them. They were as tall as Sophie and

Sam, had segmented round bodies, and as well as having two arms and two legs, had four other hairy limbs waving from their backs. Their skin was a mottled dark grey, and their red eyes gleamed on either side of their hooked noses. Two long yellow fangs curved out of each of their mouths.

Sophie could hardly get the words out. "OK.

This is officially not good."

Sam nodded. His face was as white as paper.

The creatures shifted from two legs to eight as they scuttled closer to each other. "Humanssss!" hissed the one on the left, who had particularly long fangs.

"Just when I was feeling hungry too," replied the one with jet-black legs on the right. He gave a rattling laugh and rubbed two of his legs together. "After a big fat bluebottle fly, there's nothing I like better than a human, and these two look very juicccccy indeed!"

"Stay still, little humansssss," wheedled Long Fangs, creeping closer. "We promise we won't hurt you."

"*Much!*" cackled Black Legs. "Just one bite from our fangs and then you won't feel a thing."

"Stay away from us!" Sophie said bravely. "I am the Guardian of the Gateway!"

The creatures' red eyes gleamed. "Better and better!" said Long Fangs. "So we eat you and your delicious-looking friend, and then we find the gems with no one to stop us."

"Excccccellent plan!" hissed Black Legs. "How King Ug will reward us! The Spider Gnomes will be celebrated by all shadow creatures for evermore."

Sophie's fear faded as anger flowed through her. Who did these Spider Gnomes think they were? Glaring at them, she put her hands on her hips. "Yeah, well, there's one problem with that…"

"And what's that?" chuckled Long Fangs.

Sophie flicked her ponytail back. *"Me!"*

Running forward, she jumped into the air,

turning sideways. She kicked out hard with her left foot and then her right. *Crunch! Crack!* Her feet thwacked into Long Fangs's chest and one of his legs.

"Bullseye!" whooped Sam from behind her.

Sophie leapt again, aiming for Long Fangs's head – but as she flew towards him, the Spider Gnome tensed. The next second he was jumping high in the air.

"Argh!" cried Sophie in surprise as her feet met thin air. She fell to the ground. As the breath was knocked out of her body, she felt her arms and legs being caught up behind her. "Let me go!" Sophie struggled wildly as four other limbs wrapped round her. Black Legs's grip grew tighter and tighter, until she could hardly breathe. All of a sudden she heard Sam's yell.

"Die, you eight-legged mutant spider freak!"

Sam's backpack thudded into the Spider Gnome holding Sophie. The creature hissed, and his grip loosened. Sophie's breath returned in a rush. It was all the chance she needed.

Drawing on her superstrength, she ripped the Spider Gnome's legs away from her and sprang free. Whipping through the air, she *thwacked* him solidly in the head with her foot. He screeched and crumpled to the ground. Sophie grinned in triumph. Ha! One down – at least until this one came to again!

Turning, her eyes widened in horror as she saw Long Fangs soaring through the air. "Sam! Watch out!" she shouted. Landing right beside Sam, the Spider Gnome grabbed him with his bristly legs.

"Hey!" yelled Sam.

It all happened so fast. Sophie saw the backpack fly out of Sam's hands and on to the ground, spilling out the two mega-soakers; she saw the Spider Gnome raise his head; saw his horrible fangs flash... and watched as they sank down towards Sam's neck.

4

Escape!

No, this couldn't happen! Sophie picked up one of the mega-soakers and threw it at Long Fangs. It smacked into the side of his head just as the sharp tips of his fangs scratched Sam's neck. The shadow creature snarled and pulled back in surprise.

"I can see that you still need to learn some mannersssss, little girl!" he hissed.

Sophie's heart thudded. "Yeah, well, come here and teach me some!"

"With pleassssure!"

The Spider Gnome dropped Sam and came scuttling towards Sophie. She grabbed the mega-soaker off the floor. Remembering that Sam had refilled the reservoirs just before they left his house, she blasted Long Fangs with it.

The jet of water hit the startled Spider Gnome. He reeled backwards, spluttering and hissing. "Ack! How dare you, you – you—"

Nearby, Black Legs was just starting to stir. Sophie raced to the dazed-looking Sam and thrust the mega-soakers into his hands. "Here, keep firing while I get us out of here! I've still got my superstrength."

She threw Sam over her shoulder in a fireman's lift. He didn't need telling twice. As she started to run, he fired two blasts straight at the Spider Gnomes. They screeched with rage as the water hit them, waving their bristly legs.

"You'll pay for thissss, Guardian Girl!" choked out Black Legs.

"Yessss, you and your friend will pay if it's the lasssst thing we do!" gurgled Long Fangs.

Sophie raced back through the woods, the tree trunks whizzing by. As they got closer to her house, she felt Sam grow heavier, and her strides became slower. The magic was wearing off. They reached the edge of the woods and, panting, she stopped and put Sam down.

"That was close!" Sam gasped, looking shaken. He put his hand to his neck.

"Let's see." Sophie checked it out. There was a scratch there, but nothing more. She shuddered. "I thought you were going to be properly bitten!"

"Me too." Sam stared down at the ground. "Sophie, I – I'm sorry I'm so useless."

54

"You're not useless!" Sophie exclaimed in surprise. "I'd probably have been bitten myself if you hadn't hit that Spider Gnome with your backpack. That was brilliant!"

"You still always end up having to save me though," Sam pointed out glumly.

Sophie looked at his downcast face. "What are you talking about? You're amazing to even come into the woods at all! I've got superpowers, but you're just you."

Sam made a face. "Yeah – that's the problem." He changed the subject. "Anyway, I can't believe that after all that, we still didn't find out why all the normal spiders are coming out of the wood."

"Well, I vote that we don't go back to find out!" said Sophie. "Not today, anyway."

They climbed over the fence into her garden.

"Your grandpa's going to be really mad when he hears what we did," said Sam as they headed towards the house.

Sophie hesitated. "We don't *have* to tell him, do we?"

"OK, let's not," Sam agreed quickly. "We'll just keep trying to work out the clue for the red gem. I hope we don't see those Spider Gnomes again though." He winced and rubbed the scratch on his neck. "This really hurts."

They went inside. In the kitchen they could hear Mrs B talking to Nigel. "Can you say 'Who's a lovely parrot?' Come on. Who's a lovely parrot?"

"Gimme a carrot!" squawked Nigel.

Sophie and Sam giggled and went upstairs. Their smiles faded when they saw Grandpa waiting on the landing. "Have you worked out

the clue yet?" he demanded, following them into Sophie's bedroom.

"Not quite," admitted Sophie, wondering what he'd say if he knew where they'd been. Beside her, Sam moved his hand up to hide the scratch on his neck.

Grandpa huffed. "Well, I've been looking at *The Shadow Files*. And though I found notes on some creatures called Spider Gnomes, I can't find any mention of real spiders."

"Spider Gnomes!" Sophie glanced at Sam. "What… what does it say about them?"

"That entry has been damaged."

"Can I see anyway?" Sophie asked.

Grandpa opened the book and showed them. At some point, someone had spilled a drink on the page. Even so, Sophie recognised the creatures they'd just fought in the woods.

Her eyes flicked over the words that could still be read.

Very like real spiders... Eight limbs and... Can spin web and... NB Antidote involves eating web...

Sophie stared down at the stained page. If only it hadn't been damaged! Beside her, Sam looked as frustrated as she felt.

Grandpa frowned. "As I said, it's of no use to us. There's no mention of real spiders." He shut the book. "Forget about the Spider Gnomes. I'll watch the spider situation, and you two can focus on finding the gem."

Sophie bit her lip as Grandpa strode out. She had an awful feeling that the Spider Gnomes weren't going to be quite so easy to forget!

5

Sam Behaving Strangely

he next day, Sophie spotted even more spiders as she and Sam walked to school. "I wish we'd found out why they were all coming into town like this," she said, watching them march along the pavement. "It's got to be something to do with those Spider Gnomes, but what?"

"Mmm," Sam said distractedly. He was staring at something a little way ahead of them.

Sophie followed his gaze. A blackbird was sitting on the fence. "Look at that bird," said Sam, sounding disgusted. "It looks so… *evil.*"

"Evil?" Sophie echoed in surprise. "Sam, it's just a blackbird."

Suddenly the bird flew up from the fence, swooping towards the spiders on the pavement. Sam yelped and ran forward, waving his arms. "Hey, you great big bully! Why don't you pick on someone your own size?" The bird gave a startled squawk and flew off. Sam gazed after it with a strange loathing. "Horrible thing! I bet those poor spiders were really scared."

Sophie shook her head helplessly. Her best friend was often a little bit crazy; it was one of the things she liked about him. But he wasn't usually this bad! She sighed. "Come on, Great Spider Protector – let's get to school."

Sam's odd mood continued throughout the day. In science he picked up the piece of cardboard they'd been given to do an experiment with and started smelling it!

"What are you doing?" Sophie asked in astonishment.

Sam breathed in deeply. "Mmmmm. Have you ever noticed how great cardboard smells, Soph?"

Sophie raised her eyebrows. "Um, no."

"Lovely, lovely cardboard," Sam said, happily stroking it.

"Sam!" Sophie snatched it off him before Anthony and his friends noticed. They'd tease him forever if they saw him stroking cardboard!

"*You* smell it," Sam urged. "Go on!" He grabbed her arm, trying to lift the cardboard towards her nose.

"*No!*" Sophie frowned. "Sam, are you feeling OK?"

He looked surprised. "Yes. Why?"

"Oh, no reason. I mean it's totally normal to want to smell cardboard!"

"It just smells nice, that's all," Sam protested.

Sophie put the cardboard away under her books. "You are being seriously weird today," she told him.

After school, it was time for the first meeting of the new basketball club. Sophie had persuaded Sam to join it. Sam looked glum as they all gathered in the gym. "I wish you'd just let me go home," he whispered to Sophie. "You know I'm going to be rubbish at this – I'm useless at sport!"

"You've got to at least try," said Sophie firmly. She'd been really looking forward to the new club. "You never know, you might be really good and it would be cool to have a sport we could do together."

Mr Fergus, the PE teacher, put them into teams of four. "Right!" he called, "let's see which team can shoot the ball through the hoop the most times in five minutes. Starting… now!" He blew his whistle.

Sophie was in a team with Sam and two other year-five boys, Jake and Nasim. Aiming carefully, she managed to get the ball through the hoop on her third attempt. Nasim, who was very tall, did it on his second try. Jake jumped up and down, flinging the basketball and failing each time.

Finally it was Sam's turn. Looking nervous, he dribbled the ball a few times. Suddenly, almost as if he hadn't planned it himself, he squatted then soared up into the air, so high that he was only a little bit lower than the hoop. He shoved the ball down through it with a *swish*. As Jake and Nasim whooped, Sam landed, his eyes wide with astonishment.

"Cool, Sam!" said Jake, banging him on the back.

"But – how did you do that?" Sophie gasped. She'd never seen Sam jump like that before in his life!

"I—I don't know," he stammered.

"It was *awesome*," breathed Nasim. "Do it again!"

Once more Sam sprang upwards, this time half-turning in the air as he patted the ball down through the hoop. *Woosh!* A look of excitement dawned on his face as he landed. "Oh, wow!" he burst out. "You were right, Soph. I *am* good at basketball, afterall!"

"But…" Sophie shook her head. "I don't get it. How can you be *this* good?"

"It doesn't matter. Just keep doing it!" said Nasim, looking at the other teams who were all

struggling to get the ball through the hoops.

Grabbing the basketball, Sam did it again and again. *Swish! Woosh!* Nasim and Jake cheered each time. Sophie was too stunned to join in.

Mr Fergus beamed as he came over. "Well done, Sam! I think we've found our star player. Are you *sure* you've never done this before?"

The session continued with them practising running with the ball, dribbling it and passing it. Sam was the star of the afternoon. He dodged and darted, never being caught or stopped.

At the end of the session, Sam was surrounded by a group of year fives and sixes all wanting to talk to him. Feeling worried, Sophie went to get changed. When she came out, Sam was waiting for her, smiling from ear to ear. "Thanks for making me come to basketball today, Sophie."

"Mmm." Sophie put her clothes away in her bag.

"What's up?" he said.

She hesitated. "Sam, don't you think it's just

a bit weird, you being so good at basketball? I mean, you've never even played before! You... you don't think there could be something magic going on, do you?"

Sam looked offended. "So, just 'cos I'm good at a sport for a change, it has to be magic? Thanks a lot, Sophie!" He turned away.

"Wait!" Sophie put her hand on his arm. "I'm sorry. Of course you can be good at sport. I'm just being stupid." To her relief, she saw the cross look fade from his face.

"I guess it *is* a bit weird," he admitted. "But it feels great to be good at something like this for a change!" He swung his bag over his shoulder. "Look, why don't we go into town now?" he suggested. "Maybe we'll see something that'll help us figure out the clue for the red gem."

Sophie nodded. As they left school and walked into Upper Gately, she kept darting worried looks at Sam. Despite what she'd just said to him, she still half thought something strange must be going on.

But what could it possibly be?

6

A Nasty Bug

At first glance it seemed to be a usual Monday afternoon in the High Street. Looking around though, Sophie could see that it wasn't usual at all. There were spiders everywhere! Thousands of them, creeping over all the buildings in town. Everyone they passed was talking about the tiny creatures, and the newsagent had a sign in the window: *"Town meeting tomorrow night at 8 p.m. to discuss spider problem. Please be there!"*

"What do you think they're all *doing*?" breathed Sophie, watching as a long line of spiders left the post office and marched towards the bakery.

"I don't know, but aren't they interesting?" Sam gazed dreamily at them.

Sophie groaned. "Earth to Sam! OK, forget the spiders." She waved her hand in front of his face. "We've got to find the red gem. It must be hidden someplace high. Remember the clue:

"Hours and minutes
Near clouds and sky
The red gem is hidden
Way up high."

Sam nodded. "So we need to find the tallest places in town."

They began to look and finally narrowed it down to three places: the war memorial, the church steeple and the town hall's clock tower.

Excitement fizzed through Sophie as she stared up at the clock tower. The clock on the wall had a large white face with Roman numerals all the way round. "That's it!" she burst out. "Sam, that's what the *hours and minutes* part of the clue means – the gem must be up there, in the tower!"

He nodded vaguely. "Mmm."

"How are we going to get up there to check though?" Sophie went on, frowning. The town hall was a brick building set back from the road. The clock tower was built over the entrance porch, with a small domed structure at the top of it. "It's so high."

Sam didn't say anything.

"Any ideas?" Sophie asked him.

He shook his head.

"Well, maybe Grandpa will be able to think

of something," Sophie said, wondering why Sam was being so quiet. "Why don't we go back to mine?"

"Actually... do you mind if I don't come?" Sam rubbed his forehead. "I'm not feeling too good. The scratch is hurting and my head's aching too. I must be coming down with something."

"Oh, no," said Sophie in concern. "Are you OK?"

Looking pale, Sam nodded as they started towards home. "I'm sure it's just a bug or something – I'll be fine tomorrow. We can figure out how to get up to the clock tower then."

But Sam wasn't fine the next day. When Sophie called for him in the morning, his mum said that he was ill and wouldn't be going to school. Worried, Sophie walked to school on her own. An awful thought was beginning to form in her head. Maybe Sam was ill because of the scratch. What if the Spider Gnomes had poisonous fangs? She fretted about it all day and after school raced straight back to Sam's house.

"Is Sam any better?" she asked when his mother opened the door.

"I'm afraid not," his mum sighed. "I'm sure he'd feel better if he went outside and got some fresh air, but he doesn't want to get out of bed." She ran a hand through her hair. "I was going to go to the town meeting tonight, but I can't leave him with a babysitter when he's sick. Maybe seeing you will cheer him up, Sophie. Do you want to pop up? Don't stand too close though; you don't want to catch it."

Sophie nodded gratefully and ran up to Sam's bedroom. He was lying huddled up in bed.

"You look awful!" she said. Even from the doorway she could see that his skin was a funny grey colour.

Sam nodded miserably. "I feel really hot, and the scratch on my neck is hurting."

The scratch was bright red and purple now. Sophie stared anxiously at it. *Was* the scratch the reason Sam was so ill?

"I told Mum I'd scraped it on a tree and she put some cream on it, but it hasn't helped," Sam continued. "She thinks I've got the flu, but I'm swelling up too." He pushed back the duvet to show her his tummy. He was usually skinny, but now his tummy was bulging out. "And all my legs ache," he went on, pulling the duvet back round him.

77

"*All* your legs?" echoed Sophie. "Don't you mean *both* your legs?"

Sam blinked. "Yeah, of course. Sorry, I don't know why I said *all*."

Sophie went nearer to the bed. "You really do look dreadful."

Sam's skin was even greyer than she had first thought. And something was different about his face. His nose somehow seemed more hooked, his teeth more pointed.

At that moment, a fly zoomed past. "Mmm. Yummy fly! Come here!" said Sam. He grabbed the fly from the air with super-quick speed. It buzzed furiously in his closed fingers.

"Sam!" Sophie stared. "What are you doing?"

"I want to eat it." Sam's eyes gleamed greedily. "I haven't eaten all day. I'm starving!"

78

"Sam! You can't eat a fly! You—"

Sam threw his head back and stuffed the fly into his mouth! Sophie was so shocked she was speechless for once.

Sam burped.

Sophie gazed at him in dawning horror. Of course! It all added up: his grey skin, the swelling tummy. Not to mention his dislike of birds the day before, his love of cardboard, his new talent for jumping – and now wanting to eat flies too!

"Sam," she whispered, aghast. "I don't think you've got flu – I... I think you're turning into a spider!"

7

Cobwebs for Supper

'm turning into a spider?" Sam
echoed.

"Well, maybe not a spider,"
Sophie gabbled. "Maybe a Spider
Gnome. All the things you're doing
– they're all spidery things. You're
even looking quite like a Spider
Gnome! It must be that scratch

81

on your neck. Maybe they have poisonous teeth."

Sam stared at her in shock. "Spiders often do have venomous fangs. It must be why I'm feeling so odd! What are we going to do?"

"It said something about an antidote in *The Shadow Files*, remember? It must have been talking about the antidote you need if a Spider Gnome bites you!" Rummaging in her school bag, Sophie pulled out *The Shadow Files*, and flipped to the right page. "Here it is – *Antidote involves eating web…*" she read aloud. "That's all I can make out, but at least it's easy. We need to get you some spiderweb – and fast!"

"But there's none here. Mum hates spiders and she hoovers up the webs whenever she sees them," Sam told her. "She's been hoovering all day!"

"Then let's go to my house. I saw some in my room this morning," said Sophie. "Though how will we get past your mum when you're supposed to be ill?"

"That'll be easy. Mum thinks fresh air is the best cure for any illness." Sam got out of bed and looked in his mirror. He shuddered. "She'd better not see me like this though."

He pulled on some clothes over his pyjamas. Soon he was dressed in jeans and a hoodie, the hood pulled up, and a scarf round most of his face hiding his grey skin and sharp teeth.

Sam's mum was downstairs on the phone. When Sam muttered that he was going to get some fresh air, she nodded and waved him off, hardly even glancing in their direction.

"Phew!" he muttered through his scarf as he and Sophie hurried out of the house. "Hey!"

He stared down at the pavement. "All the spiders have gone."

"Let's check it out later," Sophie said. "First we need to stop you turning into a Spider Gnome!"

They let themselves in through the front door of her house. Sam touched the door handle and spluttered. "Yuk! Lemon furniture polish! I can taste it in my mouth!"

"Mrs B's put it everywhere," said Sophie. "That's why."

"Bleurgh!" Sam said, being careful not to touch anything else.

Just then Mrs B's voice floated out of the kitchen, where she was talking to Nigel. "Say 'Who's a pretty boy then…'"

The parrot screeched, and Sam leapt straight up, almost touching the ceiling. "A bird!" he

gasped in a panic. "I've got to get out of here!"
He bolted up the stairs.

Sophie ran after him. She found him

cowering behind her wardrobe. "Sam, it was only Nigel!"

He nodded and stepped out, his cheeks red. "Sorry. I guess it's a spider thing – hearing him screech like that just really scared me."

Sophie saw that the cobwebs were still in the corner of her ceiling. "There you are! Get eating!" She started to pull a chair across so Sam could stand on it, but he didn't need it. Crouching down, he sprang into the air and grabbed the cobwebs. He landed with a cloud of white strands in his hand.

"Well, go on – eat it," said Sophie.

"I don't want to," he replied nervously.

"You've got to! You don't want to be a Spider Gnome, do you?"

Sam shut his eyes and shoved the cobweb into his mouth. "Yuk! It's gross!" he spluttered as he swallowed it down.

"But has it worked?" Sophie demanded.

Sam looked at himself in the mirror. "I don't *feel* any different."

"Maybe you need more," Sophie suggested.

Just then there was a sharp rap on Sophie's door. They jumped guiltily as it opened.

"I thought I heard you two come upstairs. I—" Grandpa broke off as he took in Sam's grey skin, and saw the remains of the cobweb in his hand. "What's going on?"

Sophie's stomach felt like it was shooting down in a lift, but there was no escape – she had to tell Grandpa the truth. She cleared her throat. "Um… Sam's sort of… turning into a Spider Gnome."

"He's what?" Grandpa's eyes stood out on stalks.

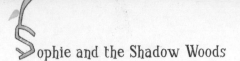

Sophie quickly told him everything that had
happened from the moment they'd gone into
the woods. "And in *The Shadow Files*, it says
the antidote is web, so we came back here to get
Sam some."

Grandpa groaned. "It won't mean normal spiderweb, you silly child. It'll mean Spider Gnome web!"

"Oh!" gasped Sophie. She glanced at Sam, who seemed to have been distracted by a bluebottle buzzing around the room. His eyes were following it hungrily.

"But I imagine you're right and Sam *is* turning into a Spider Gnome," Grandpa went on. "Many shadow creatures have venomous teeth. A single scratch from a Spider Gnome's fang could well be enough to infect a person. We must act quickly!"

"What will happen if we don't get the web?" asked Sophie in a tiny voice.

Grandpa gave Sam a grim look. "He will be a Spider Gnome forever."

Sophie bit her lip. She rarely cried, but could

feel tears in her eyes now. "It's going to be OK, isn't it?" she begged Grandpa.

"We're in this together," he told her firmly. "We'll do whatever it takes to save Sam. Understand?"

Sophie nodded hard, wiping her eyes.

"Right," Grandpa continued. "We can't let Sam go home while he's in this state. I'll ring his mum, tell her he's feeling much better and ask if he can stay for a while. Then I'll go into the woods and get some Spider Gnome web."

"But what if the Spider Gnomes attack *you*, Grandpa?" Sophie said anxiously.

Grandpa looked huffy. "I think I can manage a few Spider Gnomes, child! I might not have the powers of the Guardian any more, but I'm not quite past it yet. I have been honing my fighting skills for over fifty years!"

"But—"

"No buts. Here, take my mobile," said Grandpa, handing her his phone. "I've got a spare one in my room that I'll take with me – the number's programmed under *'Emergency'* if you need to ring me. While I'm out you must keep Sam's problem a secret. Do you think you can do that?"

Sophie glanced at Sam just as he grabbed the bluebottle out of the air and swallowed it. She winced. "Um, sure," she gulped. "No problem at all!"

Luckily, Sam's mum was only too relieved to hear that he was feeling better, and agreed to him staying longer at Sophie's. Grandpa set off, leaving Sophie in charge of Sam. She was very glad that Anthony was at a friend's house, which meant that she only had to keep Sam away from Mrs B. They stayed in Sophie's room, even though Sam wanted to go outside.

"It's horrible in here!" he said unhappily. "Every time I touch something I taste lemon furniture polish in my mouth."

"But we can't go out," Sophie told him. "What if Mrs B sees you?"

"We could go to the bottom of the garden."

"Sam, even the way you move – you're... you're scuttling," she told him.

"Am I?" Sam got up and had a go at moving across the floor. He darted sideways very fast and suddenly ran up Sophie's wall on his hands and feet!

"Get down!" Sophie exclaimed. As he dropped to the floor, her throat felt tight. If Grandpa didn't get back soon with the web, it might be too late!

Sam seemed to realise it too. They stared at each other in horror. Swallowing hard, Sophie started to say something, but Sam put his hand up. "Shh!" he hissed, glancing upwards.

Sophie blinked. "What is it?"

"Don't you hear that?"

"Hear what?"

"Whispering! Almost like…" Sam frowned, his eyes scanning the ceiling. "Sophie!" he said in a low voice. "There are two spiders up there – and I can understand every word they're saying!"

8

The Spider Gnomes

Sophie gaped upwards. Two spiders were now in the cobwebby corner, huddled close together. "You can understand them?" she repeated weakly.

"Yes, they're talking about the Spider Gnomes," Sam whispered. "The reason there have been so many spiders about is that the Spider Gnomes sent them into the town like spies, to see if they could find the gem. And the reason the spiders have all suddenly vanished—" He stopped, going pale.

"Yes?" demanded Sophie.

"... is because they've found the red gem, and now they've gone to tell the Spider Gnomes!" Sam breathed. "It *is* at the top of the clock tower, just like you thought yesterday. The Spider Gnomes are on their way to get it right now!"

Sophie's blood ran cold. "Oh, no! If they get the gem then they'll open the gate, and let all the shadow creatures loose into our world!"

Sam grabbed his bag. "Come on, we have to stop them!"

Then Sophie realised. "But *you* can't go. Sam,

you've got to wait here for Grandpa to get back with the web or you might be a Spider Gnome forever."

Fear crossed Sam's face, but then he shook his head firmly. "I'm not letting you fight those things alone, Sophie! Besides, I bet I could really help you, now I'm like this. I could be of use for once!"

Sophie wavered. She knew she needed all the help she could get.

"Sophie, we can't stand here debating all night!" insisted Sam, flipping his hood over his head again. "I'm going, all right?"

Sophie took a deep breath. "All right."

They slipped downstairs. In the kitchen, Sophie could still hear Mrs B chatting to Nigel. As quietly as she could, she went to the cupboard under the stairs and took out the

lemon furniture polish.

Sam looked horrified. "What are you doing? That stuff's disgusting!"

"Exactly," whispered Sophie as she tucked it into her rucksack. "And I bet the Spider Gnomes won't like it either!" Closing the cupboard door, she quickly scribbled a note to Mrs B, saying they had just popped round to Sam's to fetch some homework.

"Right," she said. "Let's go!"

When they reached town, the streets were very quiet. At first Sophie couldn't think why, and then she remembered the town meeting. Sure enough, the town hall was lit up inside, as everyone gathered to complain about the spiders. *They haven't even noticed that the spiders are all gone now!* thought Sophie.

She stared anxiously up at the clock tower. "How are we going to climb up there without anyone inside hearing us?"

Sam grinned. "Just leave it to me!" With a sudden spring, he leapt on to the side of the building and scuttled silently upwards, so fast that he was just a blur. A second later, he was standing in the little domed structure above the clock face.

"Do you see the red

gem?" hissed Sophie.

Sam was searching, poking around. "No, I don't see it anywhere… No, wait – yes!" His voice became excited. "It's right behind the clock! I lifted up a sort of trapdoor, and now I can see it down there, glowing in the machinery."

Sophie's heart thudded. "Can you get it out?"

"Maybe… It's wedged in really tight though…" Sam's voice faded. Faintly, she could hear him pulling and tugging at something.

Sophie clutched her fists in frustration. If only she was up there with him! She knew that the two of them, working together, could get the gem out in no time.

"Sam, why don't you—" Sophie broke off as she felt her Guardian powers tingle through her.

The Spider Gnomes were nearby! She whirled in place, peering into the darkness. Where were they? "I know you're there," she said fiercely. "Come out and fight!"

"With pleassssure," hissed a dry voice.

There was a shadowy blur as Black Legs jumped towards her. Sophie leapt up. *Crack! Thump!* Her feet struck the Spider Gnome in the stomach.

"OOF!" gasped Black Legs, crashing to the ground. His jaws clicked together menacingly. "You'll pay for that!"

Inside the town hall, Sophie could hear loud arguing going on. Nobody was paying any attention to what was happening outside. "Yeah, and who's going to make me?" she demanded, reaching inside her rucksack for the lemon polish.

"Me!" gurgled another voice.

Sophie gasped as bristly legs grabbed her from behind. She'd forgotten about Long Fangs! As she kicked and struggled, Black Legs leapt forward. Holding his hands up, streams of sticky cobweb flowed from his palms. In seconds, Sophie was bound up so tightly she couldn't move.

"That should hold you!" snapped Black Legs. "Now if you'll excusssse us – we've got a gem to get!"

"Sam, watch out!" shouted Sophie as the two Spider Gnomes started climbing up the building.

"What did you say?" came his muffled voice back. "Sophie, I've almost got it – just a few more tugs—"

Argh! Gritting her teeth, Sophie called her superstrength to her, straining against the sticky strands. Harder... harder...! At first, nothing happened, and then all at once the cobwebs ripped away. *Yes!*

Grabbing the furniture polish, Sophie jumped at the wall, using her superstrength to climb up the brick as fast as she could. The Spider Gnomes were far above her. "Sam!" she

called again as they reached the top. "Watch out!"

A faint red glow lit the air. "Sophie, I've got the gem – *mmph*!" she heard Sam cry.

"We'll take that!" crowed a triumphant voice. "Thanksssss very much!"

Sophie put on a burst of speed and reached the top, hopping nimbly over the railing. But it was too late. Black Legs and Long Fangs were already gone, scuttling away down the other side of the building. Sam was just sitting up, looking dazed.

"Sophie, I had it! And then the Spider Gnomes appeared out of nowhere—"

"I know, I was trying to warn you!"

Racing to the other side of the little dome, Sophie peered down. She could just see Black Legs and Long Fangs far below scuttling

towards the Shadow Woods. A red light shone
between them. The Spider Gnomes had the
gem!

"We have to stop them!" cried Sophie. But at

the same moment, her Guardian powers faded. She clutched the railing, feeling woozy from being up so high. "Whoa!" she gasped.

"Don't worry," said Sam. "I've got you! Here, hang on!" And with Sophie clinging to his back, he scrambled down the tower.

Sophie and Sam raced through the empty streets. With his new spider speed, Sam was able to outrun Sophie, until finally she felt her body start to tingle again as the Guardian powers returned. They were catching up with the Spider Gnomes! But would they reach them in time?

Grandpa! remembered Sophie suddenly. He was already there in the woods, getting the cobweb for Sam. Maybe he could help! Taking out his phone as she ran, Sophie tried the number programmed under *Emergency*. But the call went straight through to voicemail. Sophie stared at the phone worriedly. What did *that* mean? Was Grandpa OK?

First things first, she thought grimly, tucking the phone away again. *We have to get that gem back – no matter what!*

9

A Cobwebby Encounter

ophie and Sam reached the
Shadow Woods and charged along
the overgrown path. The woods
were even darker now that it was
night-time, with only the moon
shining down through the branches
for light. The trail led them all the
way to the same massive trees

they'd seen before. The giant cobweb looked ghostly as it hung from the branches.

"Now what?" Sam whispered as they stopped in front of it.

But before Sophie could reply, Sam tensed. "They're coming! I can hear them!" He was gone in a flash. Before Sophie could react, the two Spider Gnomes dropped from the trees beside her.

"It's her again!" snapped Black Legs.

Long Fangs scuttled closer to him. "She'sssss come for the gem!"

The Spider Gnomes stood shoulder to shoulder with their glittering red eyes, waving legs and big round bellies.

Sophie glared at them. "That's right. I've come for the gem. Give it to me."

The Spider Gnomes cackled. "She thinks she

can tell us what to do!" hissed Long Fangs.

"Never. The gem is oursssssss." Black Legs pulled a gleaming red gem out of the rags of clothes on his body and held it up triumphantly. "King Ug shall use it to open the gateway!"

"Oh, no, he won't!" Sophie put her hands on her hips. "Because I'm going to stop you from giving it to him!"

"And how exactly are you going to do that?" demanded Black Legs, tucking the gem away again.

Sophie pulled the furniture polish from her rucksack. "Like this!" she said, spraying it all over them!

The Spider Gnomes hissed in horror and retreated, half falling over. "Ugh! Lemonssssss! Argh, ick!"

Sophie advanced, still spraying the polish.

Long Fangs crumpled to the ground, gasping and choking. Then there was a spluttering noise as the polish ran out. Sophie caught her breath. *What now?*

Black Legs seemed to be recovering. "Problemsssss, little girl?"

"You wish!" Throwing the can aside, Sophie spun round, her legs whipping through the air. Her feet smacked into Black Legs's chest, sending him sprawling backwards. The red gem spilled out of his pocket and tumbled across the ground. Sophie lunged forward, her fingers closing over it.

"Oof!" The wind was knocked out of her as Black Legs leapt at her.

"Give me that gem!" he snarled. She saw his pointed teeth, the dark tunnel of his throat. As his fangs descended, she threw herself to one

side, rolling over. Black Legs jumped after her, but suddenly there was a loud crack and the Spider Gnome was thrown backwards, hit by something swinging from the trees.

"*Geronimo!*" yelled Sam as he swung past on a web rope that seemed to come from his hands. He landed in the tree opposite. "Got him!" He turned to Sophie with a grin. "That's another good thing about almost being a Spider Gnome – I can make web now!"

Sophie jumped up with the gem.

"No!" Black Legs hissed as he spotted it in her hand.

"Let me see… um, yes!" Sophie teased, holding it out before snatching it back.

"Behind you, Soph!" shouted Sam. But it was too late. Long Fangs was running at Sophie from behind. Suddenly spiderweb hit her from two directions as Black Legs and Long Fangs both blasted her.

"Are you all right, Sophie?" yelled Sam.

"Mmpph!" Sophie couldn't reply, the sticky

web was all over her. This was even worse than before! Calling her superstrength to her, she struggled as hard as she could. The web didn't budge.

The Spider Gnomes looked up at Sam. "We'll get you in a minute, boy," snapped Black Legs. "First, the gem!"

Black Legs and Long Fangs closed in on Sophie. With a battle cry, Sam swung down fast through the trees again and kicked out, knocking both of them to one side this time.

Finally Sophie tore free of the web. "Come on, Sam!" she gasped. "Let's get out of here!"

"You might want to think twice about that!" snarled Black Legs as they turned and raced down the path. "Haven't you wondered where your grandfather is?"

Sophie stopped and swung round, an icy

feeling running down her spine. "What do you mean?"

With a cackle, Long Fangs pulled back the curtain of cobwebs, and to Sophie's horror, she saw a person-sized cocoon made of web, swinging from a tree. Two blue eyes stared out desperately.

"Grandpa!" Sophie cried.

10

Run For Your Lives!

Long Fangs gave an evil grin. "Yessss, we were on our way to King Ug when we found him snooping around... and so we decided to stop and have a little fun."

"Want him back, do you?" said Black Legs, his eyes glinting meanly.

"Then you'd better give us the gem!"

Sophie looked at Sam in despair. "What are we going to do?" she whispered. "We've got to rescue Grandpa!"

Sam shook his head. "But how? We've run out of spray!"

"If only we had something that would really frighten them," Sophie groaned.

Sam's eyes suddenly widened. "That's it, Soph! Keep them talking! I've had an idea!" Before Sophie could say anything, Sam grabbed something from her pocket. "I'm out of here, Soph!" he yelled loudly so the Spider Gnomes could hear. "You're on your own!" And, jumping into the bushes, he was gone.

The Spider Gnomes cackled. "Desssserted!" sneered Black Legs.

"Left all alone!" cackled Long Fangs. "Though he'll be back when the venom has finished its work. Then he'll be one of us. Now give us the gem, little girl, or we and your friend will have your grandfather for sssssupper!"

Sophie swallowed hard. Grandpa was struggling, trying to shout, but the web was wrapped tightly round his whole body and head. He looked like an Egyptian mummy.

"Bring it here!" Black Legs beckoned her with one bristly leg.

Sophie walked slowly forward. How could she possibly free Grandpa and escape with him and the gem? And where *had* Sam gone? *Keep them talking*, he'd said. He obviously needed some time for something. But what?

She stopped in front of the Spider Gnomes.

"The gem," Black Legs hissed.

"Get my grandpa down first," said Sophie, trying to stay calm.

Black Legs nodded at Long Fangs, who scuttled in through the cobwebs. In seconds he had scuttled up the tree and sheared through the cobweb rope holding Grandpa with his teeth. Grandpa fell like a stone, but luckily the cocoon cushioned him. Sophie could hear him trying to shout as he bounced on to the forest floor.

"Now give us the gem," said Black Legs.

Grandpa desperately shook his head. Sophie hesitated as the Spider Gnomes took a step closer to her. She could try and fight them, but what if one hurt Grandpa while she was fighting the other?

Think. Think.

"The gem!" Black Legs's voice grew angrier. He nodded at Long Fangs, who grabbed Grandpa and bared his fangs. He brought them down to Grandpa's neck.

"No, don't!" Sophie gasped. Whatever Sam's plan was, it was too late. "You can have the gem! Here!" But even as she pulled the gem out of her pocket, a faint screeching noise could be heard, high up in the trees.

Nigel! Sophie thought instantly. But how could it be? Even with his new spider speed, Sam couldn't have reached her house, got the parrot without Mrs B noticing, and returned by now. It was impossible!

Both Spider Gnomes tensed and looked up. The screeching sound was getting louder with every second. It sounded like a parrot was flying through the trees – and not just any parrot, but a giant one!

"There's a bird coming!" yelled Black Legs.

Long Fangs started to run round in panicked circles. "A massive one!"

"Quick! Take cover!" Sophie shouted. Maybe she didn't know exactly what was happening, but she knew this was her chance to rescue

Grandpa! "It *is* a bird! I'd know that screech anywhere. It's a Greater African Spider Catcher!"

"ARGH!" both the Spider Gnomes shouted.

"A *Giant* Greater African Spider Catcher!" cried Sophie for good measure. "They eat rats and foxes, but most of all *giant spiders*!"

"EEEK!" shrieked the Spider Gnomes as the screeching came closer.

"Run!" Sophie shouted to them. "Run for your lives!"

The noise was so loud now, Sophie almost expected to see a real giant bird swooping in. "There it is! I can see it!" she pretended, pointing through the trees. "It's coming!"

"Noooooooooo!" yelled the two Spider Gnomes. Dropping down on to all eight of their legs, they began to scuttle away.

"The Spider Gnomes are over here, bird!" shouted Sophie.

The Spider Gnomes yelled louder and picked up even more speed. Their shouts gradually faded as they disappeared into the depths of the woods.

Sophie covered her ears with her hands as the bird shriek grew even louder. For a moment she saw something flash and then suddenly Sam came swinging down to the ground on a rope of web, clutching Grandpa's silver mobile phone. And out of the phone came the sound of a parrot screeching!

Sophie gasped. Of course! The mobile was playing the recording she had made of Nigel on the day Mrs B had first collected him! She'd completely forgotten about it.

Sam landed beside her and hit the off button.

The screeching stopped. "Ha! I think my idea worked!"

"Oh, wow!" Sophie was so stunned she could barely get the words out. "That was a totally brilliant plan, Sam!"

"You made me think of it! It was when you said that you wished we had something to really frighten them – I remembered how terrified I'd been when Nigel screeched in the kitchen. I knew I didn't have time to go back and get him, but then I remembered about this." Sam held up the phone. "I was hoping just the sound of it with the volume all the way up would be enough to scare the Spider Gnomes away."

"And it was!" Sophie exclaimed. "I was just about to give them the gem, but you frightened them off. You saved the day, Sam!"

Sam looked delighted. "Hey, I wasn't useless for once."

"You're never useless," Sophie told him, beaming. "You're the best!"

She heard a muffled shouting noise behind them. "Grandpa!" Running over, she started to

pull off the web, but now that her powers were fading it wouldn't budge.

"Here, let me!" said Sam. Crouching down, he used his pointed teeth to rip the cobweb away. Grandpa began to fight his way out.

"I'm free!" he gasped.

"Oh, Grandpa!" Sophie flung her arms round his neck. "I'm so glad you're OK. What happened? How did they catch you?"

Grandpa ran a hand over his head. "They heard me coming through the woods. They pounced on me before I had a chance to defend myself." He shook his head. "I didn't stand a chance. I should have thought it through more."

Sophie couldn't resist. "You know that's your problem, Grandpa; you're always just rushing in without thinking." She gave him a cheeky grin.

Grandpa fixed her with a don't-push-your-luck look. "Is now the time to tell you off for using my mobile to make recordings without asking, Sophie?"

"Hey, look at me!" Sam interrupted them.

They turned. Sam's stomach was shrinking, his teeth were turning back to normal and the grey tone was fading from his skin.

"It's the web!" said Grandpa. "You must have eaten some of it when you were freeing me. The antidote's working!"

Sam punched the air. "Hooray!" He tried to jump, but only managed a normal height. "Oh, dear, looks like Mr Fergus has lost his star basketball player!"

"What are you going to do about that?" Sophie asked. "He's going to notice if you're suddenly not as good as you were."

126

"I just won't go to the club any more. I'll say I've decided it's not my thing." Sam grinned. "It'll be cool. If I never play it again, no one will ever find out I'm not actually a basketball ace after all."

Sophie smiled. Astonishingly, it really did look like everything was going to be fine. The Spider Gnomes had gone, Grandpa was free, Sam was turning back to normal *and* they had the red gem. Its red light winked at her as she tucked it into her pouch, and then she linked arms with both Sam and Grandpa.

"Come on," she said happily. "Let's go home."

There was no trace of the Spider Gnomes as they made their way through the woods. "I doubt we'll see them again," said Grandpa as they reached the house and went into the kitchen.

"And if we do, the Giant Greater African Spider Catcher will soon scare them away!" said Sophie.

Grandpa rubbed his short hair. "Right, I'm off to take a shower. I still feel sticky from the web." Heading for the door, he stopped and turned, his eyes suddenly serious. "You two should be very proud of yourselves," he said. "Even without a chance to plan, you were a real team today. If it hadn't been for both of you, I might not be here now."

Sophie felt a warm glow. Embarrassed, she said, "Anytime you need saving, Grandpa, just call on us!"

"I'm not planning on making a habit of it." Grandpa smiled, his eyes catching hers. "Thank

you, child. I mean it."

"You know, I don't think he wishes Anthony was the Guardian any more," said Sam after Grandpa left the room.

Sophie breathed out in a happy rush. "And now there are just three gems left to find."

"We'll get them," declared Sam.

Sophie nodded. "Yeah. If we can defeat the Spider Gnomes we can defeat anything. Nothing's going to stop us!"

Sam held up his hand and Sophie met it in a high five. Catching sight of the parrot's cage, she went over. "I'm so glad you thought about using Nigel's screeches today." She lifted the cover.

"FIRE!" Nigel shrieked.

Sophie grinned. "Parrots are so cool." She scratched Nigel's head. "What do you think?"

"You stink!" the parrot cackled at her.

Sam burst out laughing.

"You stink! You stink!" Nigel screeched, bobbing up and down on his perch. "I think you stink!"

Sophie hastily threw the cover back over the cage and Nigel subsided.

Sam grinned. "Parrots really *are* cool."

Sophie laughed and nudged him. "So are adventures and I want another one! Let's go and get *The Shadow Files* and see if we can find another clue. Come on!"

Giggling together, they charged up the stairs.

11

In the Woods...

In a clearing, hidden deep in the heart of the trees, King Ug sat on his throne made out of a mouldy tree trunk. His crumbling skin was covered with dark blotches and he wore an old tattered black cloak. Three Ink Cap Goblins were bowing over and over again in front of him.

"Oh, Great King Ug!"

"Mighty King Ug!"

"Most wonderful, cunning, clever and handsome King Ug!"

King Ug preened and looked at himself in a cracked mirror. "Yes, I am looking rather good today, even if I say so myself." He tweaked a piece of flaking skin. "Now – what's the news on the Spider Gnomes? Have they fetched the gem yet?"

The three goblins exchanged nervous looks.

"Um, not quite," ventured one with a knobbly nose like a potato.

"No, not exactly," said one with particularly flaky skin.

King Ug's black eyes narrowed. "Why not?" he snapped. "They told me yesterday they knew where it was." His voice rose. "Where's the red gem?" he yelled.

The goblins each tried to push the other ones forward.

King Ug jumped to his feet. "Where is it?"

"The... the Guardian's got it!" stammered one with large feet.

"What?" King Ug stared at him.

"She fought the Spider Gnomes and won!" gasped Potato Nose.

"NO!" King Ug's roar was so loud it shook the leaves on the trees. "Compost brains! Maggot heads!" He strode towards them. They leapt out of his way, tripping and stumbling. "This cannot have happened again! Where are those Spider Gnomes?"

"Gone, King Ug!" yelped Big Feet as he was thwacked round the ears.

"But there are still three gems to find," gasped Flaky Skin from his hiding place behind a tree stump. "And there are lots of other shadow creatures we can call on."

"Lots and lots," whimpered Potato Nose. "The Snake Sprites, the Wolf Trolls, the Fire Imps…"

"GAH!" exclaimed King Ug, but there was a gleam in his dark eyes as an idea came to him. So the Spider Gnomes had failed just like the Swamp Boggles, but what if he found some really crafty creatures? A smile creased his crumbling face. Oh, yes, he knew who he was going to ask! That pesky girl Guardian might have won this time, but wait until she saw what he had in mind for her next.

He strode back to his throne, chortling. She wasn't going to like it – she wasn't going to like it at all!

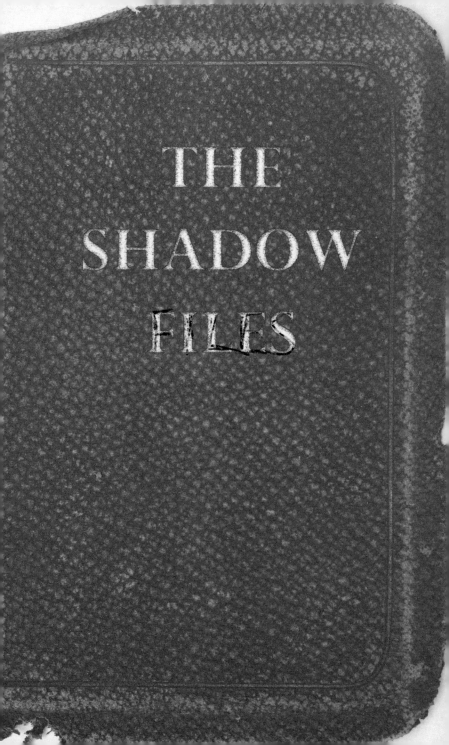

THE
SHADOW
FILES

Snake Sprites

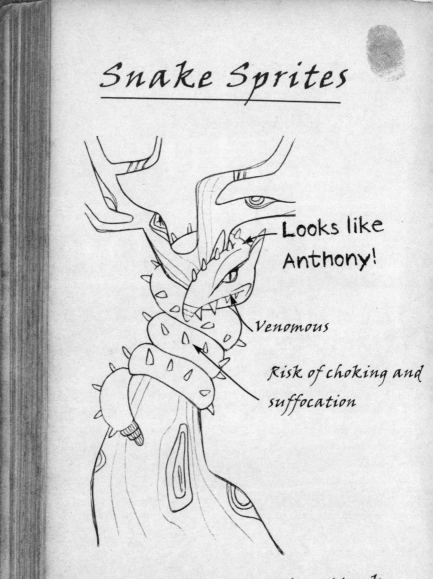

Looks like Anthony!

Venomous

Risk of choking and suffocation

Note: Snake Sprites only attack when disturbed

Habitat: Snake Sprites like to coil around the trunks of old trees

Spider Gnomes

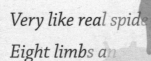

Very like real spide

Eight limbs an

Can spin web and

Antidote involves eating web

VERY SCARY!!!!

Avoid at all costs!!!!

Giant Greater African Spider Catcher

Parrots are the best!

Nature: gentle and affectionate though noisy, excellent at mimicking.
Intelligence: very clever

Food: they like nuts and seeds ... **and spiders!**

Words not to teach Nigel

What's next in store for Sophie?

Linda Chapman & Lee Weatherly

Sophie AND THE Shadow Woods

The Fog Boggarts

Only one girl can save the world...

King Ug gulped as the fog surrounded them. Before his eyes, a shiver ran through the white mist. Suddenly ten tall, thin creatures were standing there. Their skin was grey and their eyes were like large, dark holes in their long faces. Their mouths stretched almost from one ear to the other. Ug stood up straight and managed a sickly smile of greeting.

One of the creatures stepped forward, wearing a raggedy dress. Her voice was a sinister whisper. "King Ug, I am Spindle Fingers, Queen of the Fog Boggarts."

Ug inclined his head. "Greetings, Your Most Majestical Majesty."

Spindle Fingers bowed back, and then her eyes narrowed. "Your servants came to find us, King Ug. They told us you wanted our help with the little matter of finding a shadow gem. Is this true?"

Ug attempted a confident chuckle. It sounded more like a nervous cough. "Oh, that. Well, only if it's quite convenient. I mean..." He shuddered, catching sight of the queen's gaping mouth. "Yes, Your Majesty."

Her dark gaze bored into him. "We shall search all of the human world until we find where one is hidden."

Moving forward, she whipped the key out of Ug's hands. "We Fog Boggarts have many tricks up our sleeves we can use. If one way doesn't work, there are others..."

"Do you have what it takes to be the NEXT GUARDIAN?"

Prove your worth for a chance to win AWESOME prizes!
It's simple and fun!

Read the *Sophie and the Shadow Woods* series
Answer three questions about each book
Pass a stage, collect a gem, enter for great prizes/freebies
Pass SIX stages and get entered into the grand prize draw!

Stage Three

Answer these simple questions about *The Spider Gnomes*:

1. What is the name of Mrs B's parrot?
2. What does Sam start turning into?
3. What type of fruit do Spider Gnomes hate?

Got the answers? Go to:

www.sophieandtheshadowwoods.com
and continue your journey!

You can find Stage One in *The Goblin King* and Stage Two in *The Swamp Boggles*. Look out for Stage Four in *The Fog Boggarts*, out in August.

Good Luck!